This

Book Belongs to:

_____

Special thanks to Eilis, Susan, my Family & Wonderful Friends.

Illustrator Jon McCormack
Logo Design by Denise Kilroy-Toal
Printed by Winters Print, Co. Louth, Ireland

This book has been typed in Happy Sans, HFF Fourth Rock & Monumint fonts

ISBN: 978-1-9163486-0-8

First Published 2020 by Essential Marketing Ltd., 6 Park Villas, Dundalk, Co. Louth, Ireland.
E: info@essentialmarketing.ie

This edition published 2020

Printed in IRELAND

Other Books in the Vroom-Town Series:

Irish Language Versions Available:

Winner of FIRST PLACE in the Children's Picture Book Category of the Writer's Digest Self-Published Book Awards (USA)

VROOM-TOWN

by Emer Conlon

Lorcan,
Enjoy reading all about
Vabis the Scania truck!
Love
Emer & your Vroom-Town friends
xxx

The Adventure of
VABIS THE SCANIA TRUCK
and the Sleeping Volcano

It was morning time in Vroom-Town. Some of the trucks were going on an adventure with their friend, Vabis, and were very excited. They loved spending time with Vabis because he is a Scania truck with lots of cool technology and is very smart.

Screech, Sparkle, Noz and Trevor chatted excitedly together. "I cannot wait to go on our day trip with Vabis", said Noz. "I've never been on a day trip before", said Screech. "This is going to be so much fun. We will all have a great time", replied Trevor. "I doubt that", muttered Terrible Terry. He would much rather stay in Bill Byrne's yard or visit his friend, BullyDozer. Instead, he had to go away for an entire day with these trucks and Vabis. "Mmmm, how can I make this trip more interesting", he whispered to himself.

Noz cleaned and polished the trucks so much that they gleamed. He made sure that they had lots of fuel and that their tyres were pumped up. Then he checked that his laser was fully charged, in case he needed it. The trucks and Noz were soon ready to go.

Bill Byrne lined up the trucks and explained, "OK everyone, as you know you are going on a day trip to the National Park. There is a volcano there and you will be able to drive up to the top of it and maybe even take a look inside! Enjoy your day out and behave yourselves! Remember, Vabis will be waiting for you at the truck stop just outside Vroom-Town".

"Yay", said Sparkle excitedly, "I love volcanoes". BullyDozer, Daisy, Tim and Tang Arnold waved cheerio to their friends.

When Screech, Sparkle, Noz, Trevor and Terrible Terry arrived at the truck stop, they saw Vabis straight away. Vabis is a very friendly truck and he had a big smile on his face as he drove over to them. He was delighted to see his friends again. As usual, Terrible Terry was his grumpy self – he didn't even say hello.

"Are we ready to roll?" asked Vabis. "Oh yes", replied Trevor. "Let's roll", said Screech.

"Whatever", said Terrible Terry, "let's just get this over with". Sparkle and Screech both looked at him and told him not to be so rude.

Terrible Terry took the lead while the other trucks chatted and laughed together. Screech noticed a very large mountain in the distance. "Oh look at the size of that mountain, it's huge!" said Screech. "That isn't a mountain Screech, that is a sleeping volcano", said Vabis kindly.

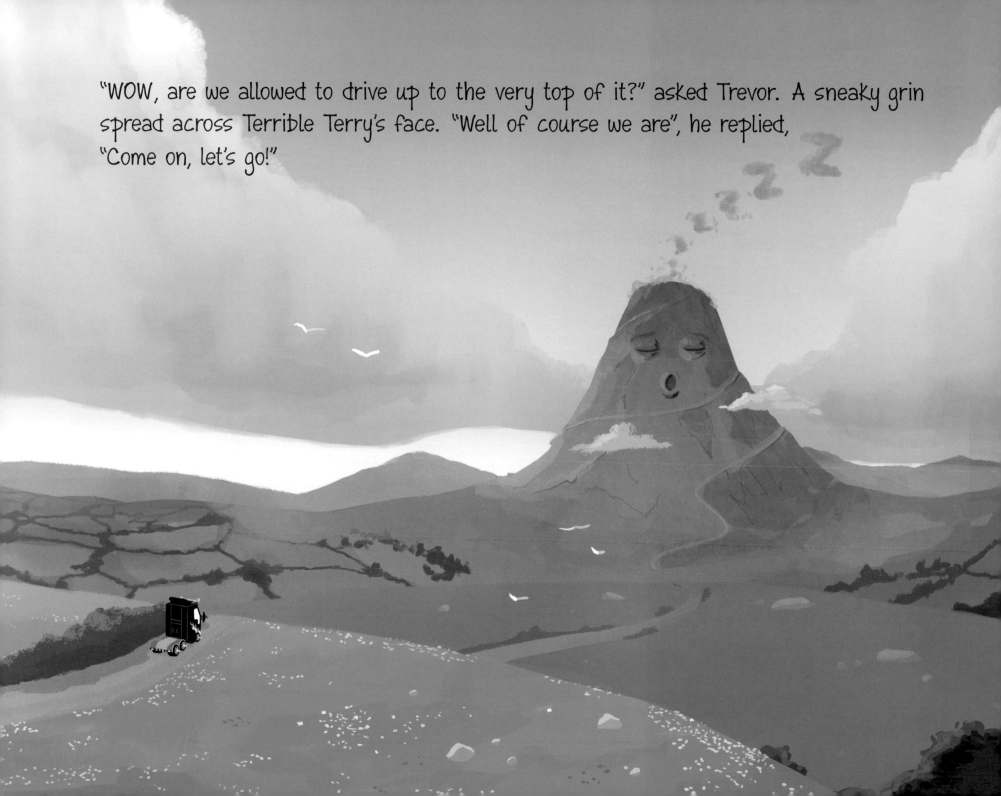

"WOW, are we allowed to drive up to the very top of it?" asked Trevor. A sneaky grin spread across Terrible Terry's face. "Well of course we are", he replied, "Come on, let's go!"

The road twisted around and around all the way up to the top of the sleeping volcano. The trucks were having great fun exploring – none of them had ever seen a volcano up close before, never mind driven around one. The view was fantastic – they could even see the Vroom-Town lighthouse in the far, far distance.

When they reached the top, they were able to look down into the volcano. "How cool is this?" asked Noz. They could see lots of different shaped rocks and when they looked really closely, deep, deep down, they could see a thick, red liquid bubbling ever so gently.

As they started to drive back down the twisty and windy road, they noticed that Terrible Terry had started to speed up a little. Then they heard a very loud scraping sound. "Look!" shouted Trevor. Terrible Terry had extended the spikes on his wheels and he was scraping them along the side of the volcano, making an awful noise. Dirt and stones were flying out from where the metal spikes were rubbing against the rock.

Suddenly, the trucks heard a low grumbling noise. "Oh no!" said Vabis, "Terrible Terry is waking up the sleeping volcano. We have to get out of here before the volcano releases hot molten lava. It will melt us if it touches us".

Terrible Terry was out of sight but they could still hear the scraping and grating noise.

The volcano suddenly opened its eyes. Now the sleeping volcano was a wide-awake volcano! The trucks heard more rumbling and grumbling. It was getting louder and louder. The lava bubbled and gurgled its way to the top of the volcano and soon it would spill over. "Oh my goodness!" cried Sparkle, "we can't seem to drive fast enough to escape".

"I have an idea", said Vabis, "my powerful V8 engine will help us. It will give us the power we need to get to the bottom of the volcano quickly and away from the lava". He unlocked some straps and asked his friends to hold on tight. The thick, hot lava began to spill and spew out over the top of the volcano.

Vabis released his handbrake and drove as fast as he could. The trucks could feel the heat coming through the sides of the volcano as they were speeding towards safety. The rumbling and the grumbling turned into a roar. Bits of rock and ash were now shooting out through the opening, flying high into the sky. "I don't think the volcano wanted to be woken up!" said Sparkle in horror.

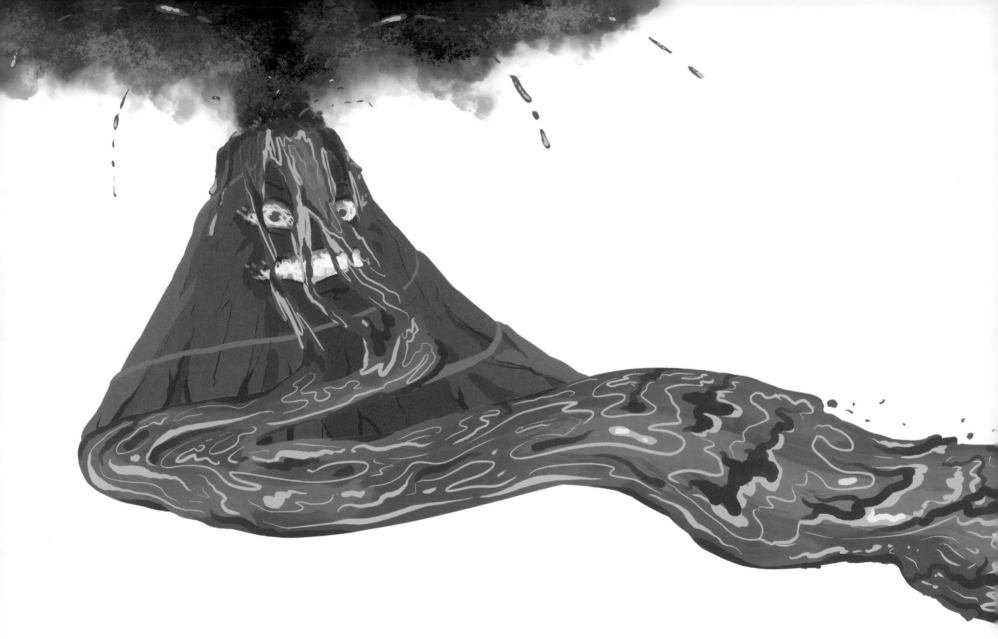

When Vabis reached the bottom of the volcano, he didn't stop. "Keep holding on everyone, it's not over yet!" yelled Vabis. The lava was creeping closer and closer towards them. The trucks could feel the heat from the lava and they were getting very hot.

"Almost there", said Vabis. He knew that if they could get a little bit further away from the base of the volcano, Noz could use his gadgets to stop the lava and then they would be safe. Vabis also knew that lava destroys everything in its path – including plants, insects and animals. It would be awful for the National Park and the environment if the lava spread too far. Vabis and Noz wanted to make sure that this didn't happen. After all, it is very important to look after our planet.

Keep holding on everyone, it's not over yet!

When they reached safety, Vabis stopped. "Right Noz, over to you", he said. Noz released his super-powerful laser and used it to create a long crack in the ground. As the thick lava reached the gap, it gurgled and bubbled down into it. Phew, the lava was back inside the earth where it belonged.

"Hurrah, we are safe!" wheezed Sparkle, "That was scary. We are so glad you were here Vabis... you saved us. Now I know why they call you *King of the Road*".

"No problem", replied Vabis, "I am happy to help. Noz did very well too – his laser gadget is super. It was great teamwork!"

"Where did Terrible Terry go?" asked Trevor. "Oh don't worry, we will catch up with him soon", replied Screech. "Let's go home", said Sparkle.

When the trucks reached Bill Byrne's yard, they could see that Terrible Terry was already on the naughty pit looking very miserable. The trucks wondered how Bill Byrne knew that Terrible Terry had done a very bold and dangerous thing.

"I suppose you are all wondering how I knew that Terry had been up to no good. It wasn't difficult", continued Bill. "I caught him sneaking through the gate and when I looked a little closer, I noticed bits of volcanic rock, ash and dirt on his spikes".

"Did he tell you about the chaos he caused?" asked Screech. "Yes, he did eventually. I put him on the naughty pit so that he can think about the danger he put you all in. He will also apologise to you for his bold behaviour". "Well, that's good", said Vabis, "we were going to tell you all about it if Terry hadn't admitted what he had done". The others nodded in agreement.

The trucks were delighted to be home and were happy to be settling into sleep mode after their busy day. Vabis was very glad to be having a sleepover with his friends in Vroom-Town. What a day... full of adventure! Let's see what tomorrow brings, he thought, as he nodded off to dreamland.

TRUCK STOP

SCANIA

GET YOUR
MARKERS!!

MAZE
FUN!

BILL BYRNE'S